Baby Parade

Jakki Wood

FRANCES LINCOLN

Wake up babies, let's start the day...

JAKKI WOOD studied graphic design at Wolverhampton Polytechnic.
She has written and illustrated many children's books
for Frances Lincoln, including *Animal Parade, Number Parade,*
Noisy Parade, Fiddle-i-fee, Bumper to Bumper,
The Deep Blue Sea and *March of the Dinosaurs.*
Jakki lives in Worcestershire.

For Polly Harding

Baby Parade copyright © Frances Lincoln Limited 2003
Text and Illustrations copyright © Jakki Wood 2003

First published in Great Britain in 2003 by
Frances Lincoln Limited, 4 Torriano Mews,
Torriano Avenue, London NW5 2RZ

www.franceslincoln.com

First paperback edition 2004

British Library Cataloguing in Publication Data available on request

ISBN 0-7112-2165-0

Printed in Singapore

1 3 5 7 9 8 6 4 2

out of bed quick, it's time to play... **We're dressed!**

Push-a-long, pull-a-long, bounce about...

peek-a-boo, pat-a-cake, let's go out... **Yippee!**

Reaching for butterflies out in the sun...

birds, bubbles, balls, let's have some fun... **Hooray!**

Pile up sand in a great big heap...

cars and trucks, brum-brum, beep-beep... **Let's play!**

Babies making lots of noise…

toot, bang, pop, we like loud toys... **Watch us!**

Dollies and teddies we like to hug...

squeeze them, cuddle them, give them love... **Aaahhh!**

Fingers, bottles, cups, plates and spoons...

whatever we're eating, it always goes soon... **Yum yum!**

Soapy bodies and bubbly hair...

slippery puddles, we don't care... Splish-splash!

Time for a story, a tickle, a hug...

lie down sleepyhead, nice and snug... **Shhhh**!

Chloe
Jessica
Jack
Amaan
Emily
Joseph
Bluebell
Molly
Kofi
Liam
Miranda
Jac

Zachary
Olivia
Lewis
Benjamin

Thomas
Luke
James
Grace
Polly
Alexan
Megan
Lauren
Clare

Martin
Sam
Matthew
Rebecca
William
Ethan
Michael
Felix
Adam
Amy
Lucy
Tyle
Aisha
Sarah

Ella
Joshua
Christopher
Ashley
Andrew
Samantha
Binisa
Reema
Callum
Tallulah
Anthony

MORE TITLES BY JAKKI WOOD
FROM FRANCES LINCOLN

ANIMAL PARADE

Go on an Alphabet Safari as 98 spectacular species go marching past.
From Aardvark to Zebra, learning your ABC has never been so wild!

ISBN 0-7112-0777-1

NOISY PARADE

Go on a Hullabaloo Safari as more than 80 animals raise their voices
in this sight-and-sound wildlife spectacular. This glorious collection
of sounds will have children hooting, quacking and howling with delight!

ISBN 0-7112-1990-7

NUMBER PARADE

Go on a Counting Safari and see the birds and beasts gain multiples
and momentum as the score mounts to 101. Complete with a lift up
surprise at the end, counting has never been so much fun!

ISBN 0-7112-0905-7

Frances Lincoln titles are available from all good bookshops.
You can also buy books and find out more about your favourite titles,
authors and illustrators on our website: **www.franceslincoln.com**